The ELEPHANTS' GUIDE to HIDE-AND-SEEK

words by Kjersten Hayes   **pictures by Gladys Jose**

Hooray for Elephant!

We love Elephant!

Play hide-and-seek with us!

Pretty-pretty-please!

sourcebooks
jabberwocky

Text © 2020 by Kjersten Hayes
Illustrations © 2020 by Gladys Jose
Cover and internal design © 2020 by Sourcebooks

Sourcebooks and the colophon are registered trademarks of Sourcebooks.

The full color art was painted digitally in Adobe Photoshop CC.

Published by Sourcebooks Jabberwocky, an imprint of Sourcebooks Kids
P.O. Box 4410, Naperville, Illinois 60567–4410
(630) 961-3900
sourcebookskids.com

Library of Congress Cataloging-in-Publication Data is on file with the publisher.

Source of Production: Wing King Tong Paper Products Co. Ltd.,
Shenzhen, Guangdong Province, China
Date of Production: December 2019
Run Number: 5017151

Printed and bound in China.
WKT 10 9 8 7 6 5 4 3 2 1

To Oscar and Lars. May you seek joy, find wonder, love big, and always choose to get in the game.
—KH

To Miranda, Jaden, and Justesse. May your days be full of fun and games, and most importantly, wonderful friendships.
—GJ

The game begins, dear elephant. But let us guess... you are the only pachyderm playing.

I'll be it!

You cannot resist the other players. You live for their happy little faces! You can't bear to disappoint them!

But no matter how much you love your friends, and how much they love this game...

...your struggle with hide-and-seek remains enormous.

You are tired of always being the largest one in the room.

You are frustrated with always being the first one found.

You love your friends, but you really, really, cannot figure out this game.

Found you!

Well, despair no more! We at the Elephant Hobby and Sport League are here to help.

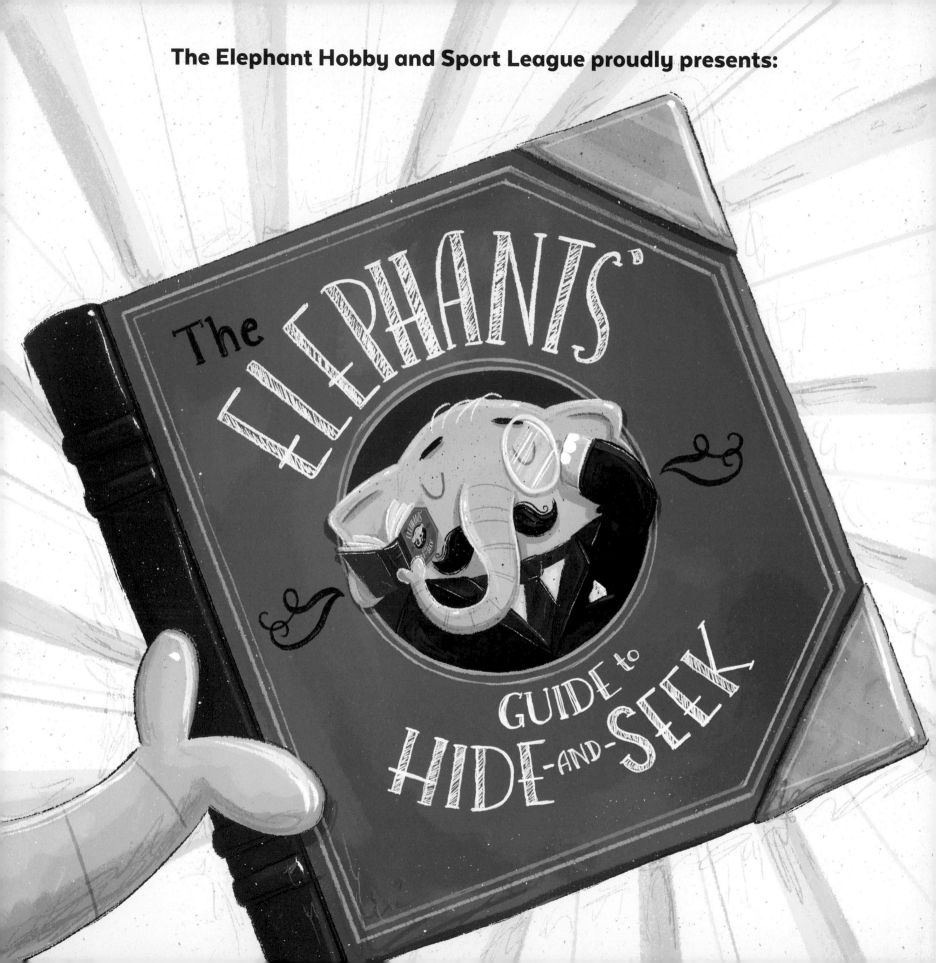

Just follow our simple, patented guidelines for hiding spaces and you WILL achieve hide-and-seek success. So what are you waiting for? Your friends are counting. It's time to get in the game.

THE GUIDELINES

Hiding behind the cushions doesn't work for us elephants.

Instead, find a room with lots of furniture and add to the collection.

Lumps in the bed are not usually elephant-sized.

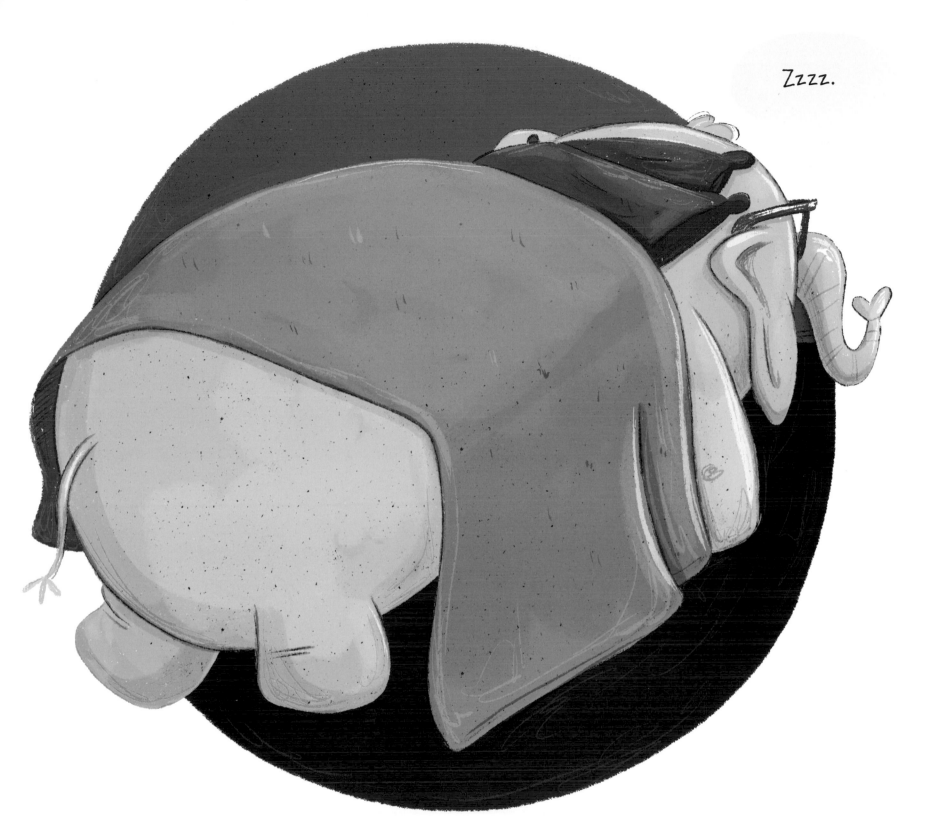

**But beds are elephant-sized! Take full advantage
of your ability to snooze while standing.**

Seek out large bathtubs with shower curtains,

**oversized tables
with long linens,**

and unsorted piles
of laundry.

Avoid china cabinets,

toy closets littered with
wheeled miniature vehicles,

and pantries overstocked with peanuts.

CRUNCH!
CRUNCH!

We elephants are especially loud when it comes to peanuts!

Think camouflage.

But beware of overdoing it.

Only choose spaces that you can get out of easily.
The bigger we elephants are, the harder we are to
get unstuck.

Make your trunk's water feature work for you.

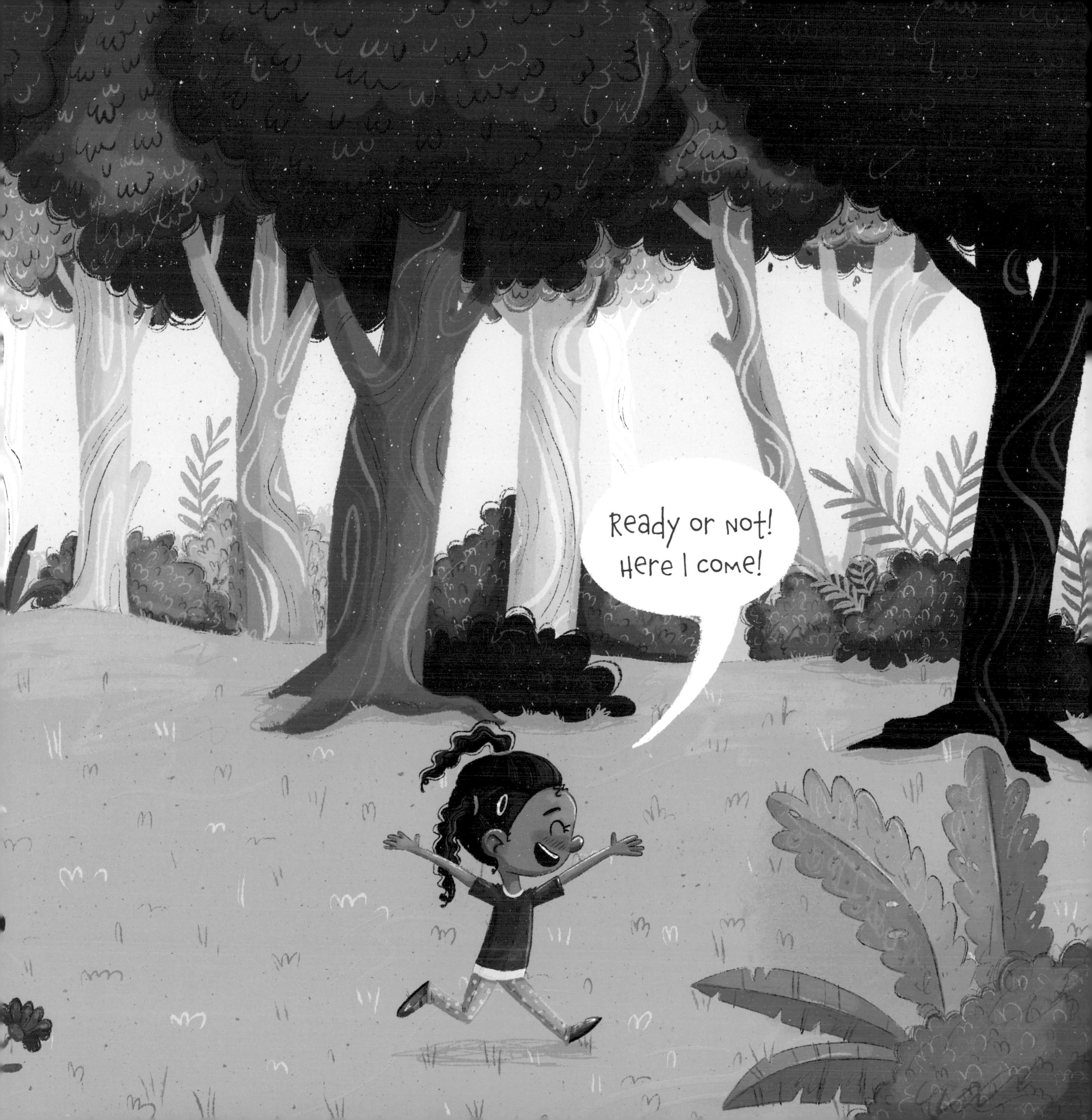
Ready or not!
Here I come!

And if all else fails...

Because, dear elephant, you love those kids! And if hiding isn't your thing...

...maybe it's not so bad to be found.